When Jesus Was A Kid Like Me

A counting song about Jesus when he was a kid like you and me.

Words and music by Mark Daniewicz
Illustrations by Steven Michels-Boyce

Beaver's Pond Press, Inc.
Edina, Minnesota

ISBN-13: 978-1-59298-106-9
ISBN-10: 1-59298-106-2

Library of Congress Catalog Number: 2005902583

Printed in the United States of America

First Printing: October 2005

09 08 07 06 05   5 4 3 2 1

Beaver's Pond Press, Inc.

7104 Ohms Lane, Suite 216
Edina, MN 55439
(952) 829-8818
www.beaverspondpress.com

to order, visit www.BookHouseFulfillment.com
or call 1-800-901-3480. Reseller discounts available.

To Colleen, Joey, Sam, & Meg;

for my Mom who just keeps humming along;

in memory of my Dad who liked my music;

and for all the kids, young and old, everywhere.

When Jesus was a kid like me,
He learned to walk and run.
He laughed and smiled and
** ran around,**
When he was only 1.

(CHORUS)

We circle 'round together now,
Hand in hand, you and me.
With Father, Son, and Spirit too,
All children of God are we.
With Father, Son, and Spirit too,
All children of God are we.

(VERSE TWO)

When Jesus was a kid like me,
He knew that it was true,
His mom and dad both
    loved him so,
When he was only **2.**

(CHORUS)

We circle 'round together now,
Hand in hand, you and me.
With Father, Son, and Spirit too,
All children of God are we.
With Father, Son, and Spirit too,
All children of God are we.

(VERSE THREE)

When Jesus was a kid like me,
He fell and skinned his knee.
It hurt. He cried.
He found his mom,
When he was only **3**.

(CHORUS)

We circle 'round together now,
Hand in hand, you and me.
With Father, Son, and Spirit too,
All children of God are we.
With Father, Son, and Spirit too,
All children of God are we.

(VERSE FOUR)

When Jesus was a kid like me,
He learned more and more,
'Bout Adam, Eve, and Noah's ark,
When he was only **4**.

(CHORUS)

We circle 'round together now,
Hand in hand, you and me.
With Father, Son, and Spirit too,
All children of God are we.
With Father, Son, and Spirit too,
All children of God are we.

(VERSE FIVE)

When Jesus was a kid like me,
He took lots of pride,
In helping out his mom and dad,
When he was only 5.

(CHORUS)

We circle 'round together now,
Hand in hand, you and me.
With Father, Son, and Spirit too,
All children of God are we.
With Father, Son, and Spirit too,
All children of God are we.

(VERSE SIX)

When Jesus was a kid like me,
He played with stones and sticks,
Like lots of kids in Nazareth,
When he was only 6.

(CHORUS)

We circle 'round together now,
Hand in hand, you and me.
With Father, Son, and Spirit too,
All children of God are we.
With Father, Son, and Spirit too,
All children of God are we.

(VERSE SEVEN)

When Jesus was a kid like me,
He looked up to the heavens,
And prayed for everyone he knew,
When he was only 7.

(CHORUS)

We circle 'round together now,
Hand in hand, you and me.
With Father, Son, and Spirit too,
All children of God are we.
With Father, Son, and Spirit too,
All children of God are we.

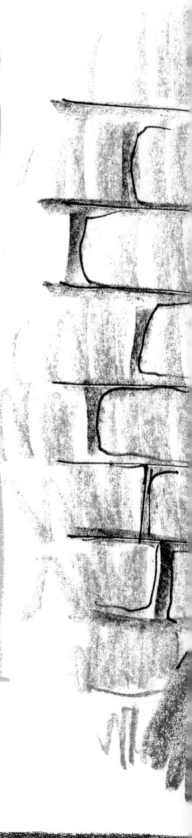

(VERSE EIGHT)

When Jesus was a kid like me,
He could hardly wait,
To go and play with all his friends,
When he was only 8.

(CHORUS)

We circle 'round together now,
Hand in hand, you and me.
With Father, Son, and Spirit too,
All children of God are we.
With Father, Son, and Spirit too,
All children of God are we.

(VERSE NINE)

When Jesus was a kid like me,
He always seemed to find,
The good in everyone he met,
When he was only 9.

(CHORUS)

We circle 'round together now,
Hand in hand, you and me.
With Father, Son, and Spirit too,
All children of God are we.
With Father, Son, and Spirit too,
All children of God are we.

(VERSE TEN)

When Jesus was a kid like me,
He liked to pretend,
The world could be a better place,
When he was only 10.

(CHORUS)

We circle 'round together now,
Hand in hand, you and me.
With Father, Son, and Spirit too,
All children of God are we.
With Father, Son, and Spirit too,
All children of God are we.

When Jesus Was A Kid Like Me

Words: Mark Daniewicz
Tune: Traditional

When Jesus was a kid like me,
He learned to walk and run.
He laughed and smiled and ran around,
When he was only 1.

(chorus)
We circle 'round together now,
Hand in hand, you and me.
With Father, Son, and Spirit too,
All children of God are we.
With Father, Son, and Spirit, too,
All children of God are we.

When Jesus was a kid like me,
He knew that it was true,
His mom and dad both loved him so,
When he was only 2. (chorus)

When Jesus was a kid like me,
He fell and skinned his knee.
It hurt. He cried. He found his mom,
When he was only 3. (chorus)

When Jesus was a kid like me,
He learned more and more,
'Bout Adam, Eve, and Noah's ark,
When he was only 4. (chorus)

When Jesus was a kid like me,
He took lots of pride,
In helping out his mom and dad,
When he was only 5. (chorus)

When Jesus was a kid like me,
He played with stones and sticks,
Like lots of kids in Nazareth,
When he was only 6. (chorus)

When Jesus was a kid like me,
He looked up to the heavens,
And prayed for everyone he knew,
When he was only 7. (chorus)

When Jesus was a kid like me,
He could hardly wait,
To go and play with all his friends,
When he was only 8. (chorus)

When Jesus was a kid like me,
He always seemed to find,
The good in everyone he met,
When he was only 9. (chorus)

When Jesus was a kid like me,
He liked to pretend,
The world could be a better place,
When he was only 10. (chorus)

If you want to teach this song, it works best to use the verses just up to the ages of the kids you're working with. Play the song a couple of times to help them get familiar with it. Once the kids have learned the chorus and a few verses, it's fun to sing this song while doing a simple circle dance.

First, form circles of from four to eight children. As they start each verse, the children hold hands and walk in a clockwise direction.

While singing the first two lines of the chorus (We circle 'round together now, Hand in hand, you and me), the circles gradually slow down and stop at "me."

Then, as each circle faces the middle, while singing the next two lines of the chorus (With Father, Son, and Spirit too, All children of God are we), they raise their hands and move into the center of the circle. When they reach the middle, everyone holds their hands high. Then, in reverse, everyone lowers their hands as they back away from the middle. When the children repeat these two lines, each circle moves into and then backs away from the center again.

When the chorus ends, the children return to walking in a clockwise direction as they start to sing the next verse.

Author's Note

Back in 1998, I found myself in charge of music for the pre-school Sunday School program at the Church of St. John in Rochester, Minnesota. My first thought was: "Why isn't there a song about Jesus when he was their age?" After I thought up the first line, the tune from an old Christmas carol ("The Seven Joys of Mary") soon came to mind. The rest came pretty easily after that.

The kids liked it, so it was a keeper. And, as we kept singing it, a fun circle dance just sort of evolved. (It turns out that people used to dance to some of these old Christmas carols back in medieval times.) Our singing circles soon moved out into the hallway, both for more room to dance and for safety's sake. Eventually, all of the classes got together in the gym, so the parents got a chance to see their kids singing and dancing too. It soon became a perennial.

Besides singing and dancing this song in classrooms, hallways, and gyms, it would be fun sometimes to do it in church too. An especially good time would be right after Christmas, when we celebrate Jesus' life with his family. The 1, 2, and 3-year-olds can sing and dance their verses with their parents. And, the 4-and-more-year-olds can each in turn sing their verses as they dance in their own age's circles. Wouldn't that be something to see? It could say something to both kids and grownups alike about who Jesus was when he was a kid and how all of us can in some ways follow in his footsteps.

Acknowledgements

For Maryann Corbett who taught me the song "The Seven Joys of Mary," which later became the melody for "When Jesus Was A Kid Like Me."

For Cate and Jerry Vockley who showed me the best way to sing the chorus. They also helped me teach the song to the kids and figure out the dance.

For the Pre-School Sunday School kids at St. John's in Rochester, Minnesota who sang and danced and taught us how to follow their lead. Our children have so much to teach us. "It is to people who are just like them that the kingdom of God belongs. I tell you, whoever does not welcome the kingdom of God like a little child will never enter it."

For Steven Michels-Boyce, who believed in this book and really made it happen with his wonderful drawings and layout. If it weren't for him, you wouldn't be reading this right now.

For Sarah Brickson, Michael Ekker, Colleen Erickson, Jared McDermott, from St. Frances Cabrini's Children's Choir in Minneapolis, Minnesota, who helped bring this song to life.

For Garry Espe (on guitar) and Steven Michels-Boyce (on standup bass), who along with my autoharp provided the musical accompaniment for the recording at Behrtrak Music with Jim Behringer.

And, for the assistance and encouragement of everyone who helped with each little step along the way so that this simple, little song could finally be shared with others.

Biographies

Mark Daniewicz is a psychologist and liturgical musician who lives and works in Woodbury, Minnesota.

Steven Michels-Boyce is an advertising art director who lives and works in Minneapolis, Minnesota.